W9-BCT-822

I Miss Franklin P. Shuckles

Story by **Ulana Snihura**
Art by **Leanne Franson**

Annick Press • Toronto • New York

Annick Press Ltd.

We acknowledge the support of the Canada Council for the Arts for our publishing program. We also thank the Ontario Arts Council.

Cataloguing in Publication Data
Snihura, Ulana
        I miss Franklin P. Shuckles

ISBN 1-55037-517-2 (bound) ISBN 1-55037-516-4 (pbk.)

I. Franson, Leanne. II. Title.

PS8587.N53I4 1998   jC813'.54   C97-932606-0
PZ7.S6802I4 1998

The art in this book was rendered in watercolours.
The text was typeset in Esprit Book.

Distributed in Canada by:
Firefly Books Ltd.
3680 Victoria Park Avenue
Willowdale, ON
M2H 3K1

Published in the U.S.A. by Annick Press (U.S.) Ltd.
Distributed in the U.S.A. by:
Firefly Books (U.S.) Inc.
P.O. Box 1338
Ellicott Station
Buffalo, NY 14205

Printed and bound in Canada by
Friesens, Altona, Manitoba.

To Daria, Marta, Roma and Taras
–U.S.

To Eleanor
–L.F.

Franklin P. Shuckles likes me.
He really, really likes me.

Franklin P. Shuckles moved in
next door during the summer.
Every day he came over and
asked if we could play.
There was no one else around.
So I did.

Franklin P. Shuckles can't throw a ball.
He has skinny legs and wears funny glasses.
Maybe that's why he can't catch either.

But he tells the best stories.

Franklin P. Shuckles always came over
and asked to play.

There was no one else around.

So I did.

I always asked him if he could tell me stories.
They were always great.
So he did.

But now he sits next to me in school all day long.

At school everyone makes fun of his skinny legs and funny glasses.

I can't be
friends with
him anymore.

Everyone
will laugh
at me too.

Maybe if I sneeze very
loud he'll move.
So I did.
But he didn't.

At lunchtime Franklin P. Shuckles always
asks if I would like to share his lunch.
Maybe if I chew very loud he'll get
grossed out and move.
So I did.
But he didn't.

At recess when I'm playing hopscotch or four square with my friends, Franklin P. Shuckles sits really close by.
I know he is looking, even though he pretends to be reading his book.

Maybe if I throw the ball at him he'll move.
So I did.
But he didn't.

After school Franklin P. Shuckles follows me home.
Sometimes he asks if he could carry my backpack.
Maybe if I make it very
heavy he'll stop asking.
So I did.
But he didn't.

Maybe if I write him a note saying
"Molly Pepper doesn't like you!" he'll
stop bugging me.
So I did.

And he did.

So now Franklin P. Shuckles doesn't sit by
me in school anymore.
Maybe if I saved him a seat he would.
So I did.
But he didn't.

Franklin P. Shuckles doesn't ask to share
his lunch with me anymore.
Maybe if I shared
my double chocolate
raisin cookies
with him he would.
So I did.
But he didn't.

During recess Franklin P. Shuckles
doesn't sit close by when I'm playing
hopscotch or four square. He sits by
the big oak tree, reading his book.
Maybe if I asked him if he'd like to
play he would.

So I did.
But he didn't.

After school Franklin P. Shuckles walks
home on the other side of the street.
Maybe if I asked him if he could help me
carry my backpack he would.
So I did.
But he didn't.

Now Franklin P. Shuckles plays
with the boy across the street.
They play catch and Franklin P.
Shuckles reads him his stories.
Maybe if I go over and ask if I
can play with them he'll let me.
So I did.
But he didn't.

Franklin P. Shuckles doesn't like me anymore.

And I feel really, really sad.
Maybe if I wave to him he'll wave back.
So I did.
But he didn't.

I miss Franklin P. Shuckles.
I miss his skinny legs, his funny glasses,
his great stories.

But most of all I miss
his friendship.

Maybe if I write him a note saying "Molly Pepper would like to be your friend again!" he would.

So I did.
And he did.

Now Franklin P. Shuckles and I are friends. I teach him games to play. And he tells me great stories. Maybe if we shook hands on being friends forever we would.

So we did.
And we are.